A Dot Markers & Paint Daubers Kids Activity Book

Learn as you play: Do a dot page a day

Farm Animals

14 Peaks Creative Arts

GOATS

COW

MOUSE

Chicken

Milk Cow

horse

Baby Chick

Donkey

FARM CAT

Bull

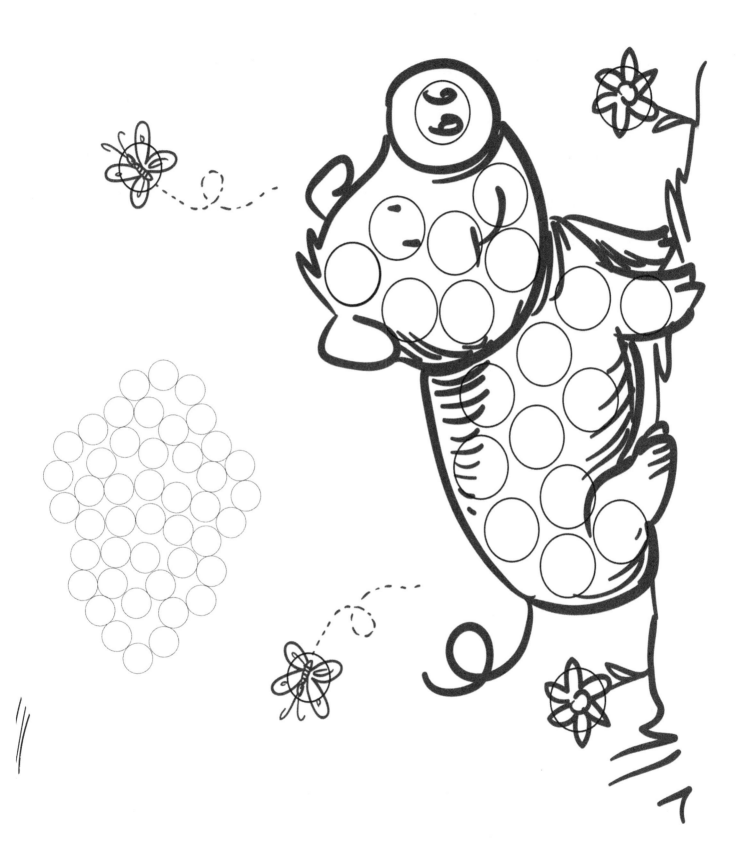

Excerpt from our Dot Marker Book

Trucks and Cars

Exclusively on Amazon

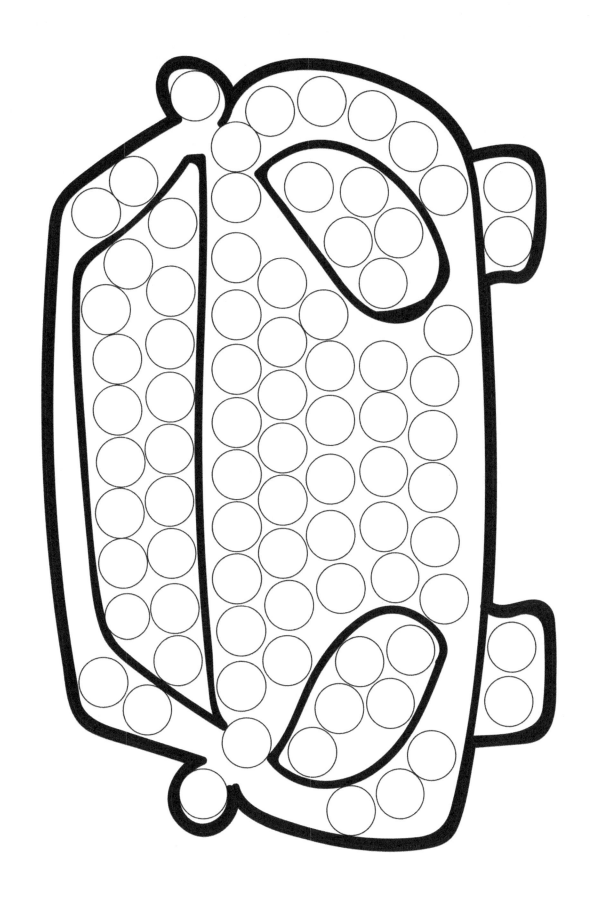

Excerpt from our Dot Marker Book

Cute Bugs

Exclusively on Amazon

Excerpt from our Dot Marker Book

Number Dots

Exclusively on Amazon

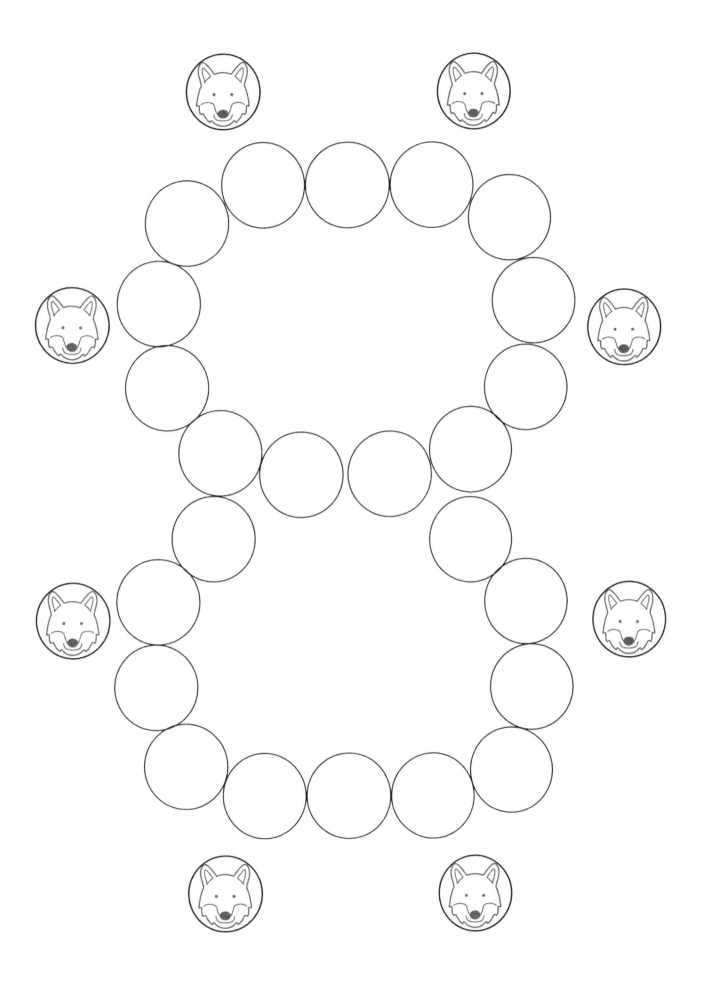

Chapter 1

A Colorful Beginning

This book began quite by accident. You see, my misfortune has become your fortune. Here's how…I was so excited, I couldn't stand it! For the first time in a long time, I had made up my mind I was going to take some time out for myself. I was a stressed-out mess, in need of some serious "me" time. Finally, I was going to do something constructive about me.

My favorite thing to do is to write, but since that is also my full-time job, that simply would not do. I set about to find something equally as fun. That's when it happened. I was at the checkout stand at the local grocery store and there it was, on the shelf…a coloring book for grown-ups.

I set about to find free color page downloads. Easy enough, right? Wrong! What seemed to be an easy, breezy task left me more stressed out than ever. In fact, it really left me blue. The first thing I encountered was that when searching for free downloads, I assumed the results that came up were going to be…free. But such was not the case. Oh no…far from it!

I spent the first day sifting out the "free" sites that wanted me to give them my credit card number. Not being a fan of dishing out my information when something is supposedly "free", I had to find a better way.

Well, finally I did find some sites that were really and truly free. One of them, however, gave me way more than I bargained for. The following few days were spent ridding my computer from a virus encountered from one of those "free" sites.

Color Yourself Lucky!

Yup! You read it right. Color yourself lucky because when I set out on a mission, you might as well consider it done. My frustration led to determination and sure enough, one by one, I found them.

Now, I have not only paved the way for you to find free (really free) downloadable coloring pages, I have gone so far as to write a book that lays it all out so you too can find hassle-free downloads for printable coloring pages.

What's more is that I make sure:

- The links work.
- The pictures are high-quality.
- There is a great variety of pages.
- To carefully categorize so you can easily jump to whatever section or sections interest you.
- This book is updated often so you stay posted on any changes.

Animals

Cuddly and cute, animals are always a favorite for children to color. The sites chosen are unbearable easy so you and your youngster can concentrate on the adorable pictures rather than going on a hairy ride with some savage beast and getting malware or a virus on your computer. Have a pawsitively great time coloring safe print outs from these trusty sites.

1. Coloring.ws.com is a nice, tame site to find adorable animals for your child to color. You will be able to choose from a whole pack of animals like llamas, horses, dogs, rabbits and rays. Oh rats! Did I forget to mention rats too? Navigation is easy too. There is no malicious activity that we found.

2. Crayola.com will not be left out of the fur-filled fun. Find animal pages that will delight and excite your youngster. You can download a single animal page or opt for an animal activity page instead. There are other things your child can do on Crayola.com too. This site is packed with fun for all.

3. For huggable animal character pages, go to Kinder Art (http://www.kinderart.com/kindercolor/farm.shtml) for a fun day on the farm. Designed for the younger ones, this site features mother and baby pictures and other adorable pictures that is almost as good as a day on the actual farm. Your tot is sure to have a hay day with these animal coloring pages.

4. Leave it to Science Kids (http://www.sciencekids.co.nz/pictures/coloringpages/animals.html) to come up with great animal picture pages that teach your child as well. Whether your adventurous one wants to opt for wild beasts or go with the huggable, furry type, this site has just about every kind on earth...and in the sea. You will notice some ads flying around. Just don't click unless you want to be redirected. The ads are harmless, just a bit obnoxious.

5. Lions and tigers and bears...oh my! Coloring Pages Kids (http://www.coloring-pages-kids.com/animals/) is a jungle full of animals to print and color. There are over 1,000 animals to choose from like tigers, owls and bunnies. You will also find insects like bees and sea creatures, swimming turtles and fish. You can choose your child's education level too.

6. If you want simple and easy. Coloring Book Fun (http://coloringbookfun.com/animals.html) offers exactly that. With a nice lion-up of animals to choose from, your child will enjoy hours of fun.

Read the rest of *Click and Color: Free Printable Coloring Pages*

And get links to 1000's of free coloring pages.

You can find it in paperback at…

https://www.amazon.com/Click-Color-Printable-Coloring-coloring/dp/1541256565

or have a free pdf delivered directly to your computer at

www.14-peaks.com

36785610R00040

Made in the USA
Middletown, DE
18 February 2019